...givers,

... are designed to provide ... experiences, as well as opportunities to develop vocabulary, literacy skills, and comprehension. Here are a few ways to support your beginning reader:

- Talk with your child about the ideas addressed in the story.
- Discuss each illustration, mentioning the characters, where they are, and what they are doing.
- Read with expression, pointing to each word. You may want to read the whole story through and then revisit parts of the story to ensure that the meanings of words or phrases are understood.
- Talk about why the character did what he or she did and what your child would do in that situation.
- Help your child connect with characters and events in the story.

Remember, reading with your child should be fun, not forced. Each moment spent reading with your child is a priceless investment in his or her literacy life.

Gail Saunders-Smith, Ph.D.

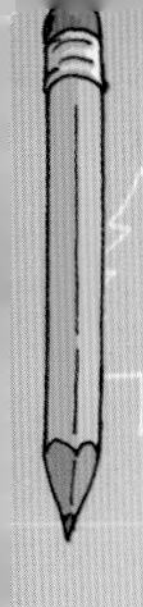

Stone Arch Readers
are published by Stone Arch Books
a Capstone Imprint
1710 Roe Crest Drive
North Mankato, Minnesota 56003
www.capstonepub.com

Library of Congress Cataloging-in-Publication Data
Klein, Adria F. (Adria Fay), 1947-
Sammy Saw and the campout / by Adria Klein ; illustrated by Andrew Rowland.
p. cm. -- (Stone Arch readers--tool school)
Summary: Sammy Saw and the Tool Team are going camping.
ISBN 978-1-4342-4022-4 (library binding) -- ISBN 978-1-4342-4234-1 (pbk.)
1. Saws--Juvenile fiction. 2. Tools--Juvenile fiction. 3. Camping--Juvenile fiction. 4. Helping behavior--Juvenile fiction. [1. Saws--Fiction. 2. Tools--Fiction. 3. Camping--Fiction. 4. Helpfulness--Fiction.] I. Rowland, Andrew, 1962- ill. II. Title.

PZ7.K678324Sap 2012
[E]--dc23

2011049284

Reading Consultants:
Gail Saunders-Smith, Ph.D.
Melinda Melton Crow, M.Ed.
Laurie K. Holland, Media Specialist

Designer: Russell Griesmer

Printed in China
032012
006677RRDF12

Sammy Saw and the Campout

by Adria Klein illustrated by Andy Rowland

Tia Tape Measure

Hank Hammer

Sammy Saw
Sophie Screwdriver
10 x 8"
8 x 14"

Sammy and his friends are going camping. Sammy packs his sleeping bag and pillow.

He also packs bug spray and
a flashlight.

“I’m ready,” says Sammy.

“Just in time,” his mom says. “Your friends are here.”

"Let's go!" says Sammy.

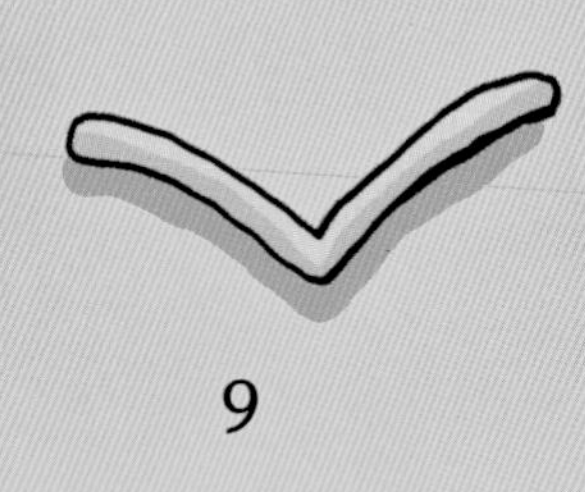

They drive and drive and drive.
They sing songs, eat snacks, and
play games.

“Look! We’re here,” says Sammy.

“Hooray!” everyone yells.

“What should we do first?” asks Tia.

“We should set up the tent,” says Sammy.

“Let’s do it, Tool Team!” says Hank.

"The tent is up," says Sammy.
"Now what should we do?"

"You can help make dinner,"
says Sammy's mom.

“We will need a fire to make dinner,” she says.

“And we will need wood for the fire,” says Hank.

“That’s right,” she says. “Be careful out there.”

“We will, Mom,” says Sammy.

The friends look all over for wood.

“I found a big log,” says Sophie.

“It’s too long,” says Hank.
“We’ll have to cut it.”

"I can measure it," says Tia.

"Hank and I can hold it," says Sophie.

"And I can cut it!" says Sammy.

Saw, saw, saw. Cut, cut, cut.
Sammy works hard.

“Not too short. Not too long. Sammy, you are cutting it just right!” says Hank.

“Let’s load up this wood,” says Sammy. “I’m getting hungry.”

The Tool Team goes back to the campsite.

“Here’s the wood,” says Sammy.

“Perfect,” says his mom. “Now let’s get cooking!”

The Tool Team puts the wood in
a pile. Mom starts the fire.

She cooks the food over the fire.

Everyone roasts marshmallows after supper. Then they tell stories around the fire.

“I like camping,” says Hank.

“Me, too!” says Tia.

“Can we go camping again next weekend?” asks Sammy.

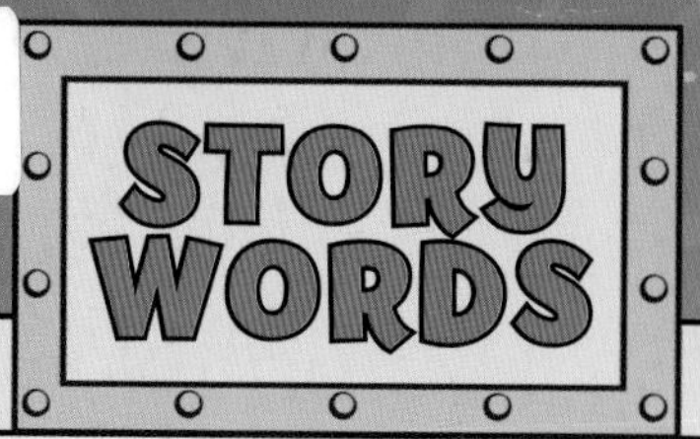

camping	drive
sleeping bag	measure
pillow	hungry
flashlight	marshmallows

Total Word Count: 286